MOJANG

MINECRAFT

GHAST IN THE MACHINE

MORGAN

ASH

HARPER

Prologue

WHO'S HONKING NOW?!

A figure stood in a darkening forest.

She was all alone. At first, that had been exciting. But as the sunlight faded, the woods grew more sinister.

There were noises in the distance: sounds of shuffling. **A strange, deep-throated honk.** She didn't know what was making those sounds, and she didn't care to find out.

She needed to leave. And that meant finding the portal. It was nearby, somewhere among the trees.

But all the trees looked the same.

She'd been turned around.

Those noises were coming closer.

The woods were getting darker.

And she knew with utter certainty that **she was no longer alone.**

Chapter 1

STAY IN SCHOOL!
UNLESS IT'S FULL OF
WITHER SKELETONS.
THEN YOU CAN LEAVE.

Jodi Mercado's mouth hung open with amazement. **She was walking the hallways of Woodsword Middle School,** just as she did on most days. She saw the bench where she drank her milk every morning. She saw the trophy case in the lobby and the colourful bulletin board just outside of Doc Culpepper's classroom.

It was all so familiar. But Jodi *wasn't* at Woodsword Middle School. Not really.

She was inside a copy. A fake. It was a life-size re-creation of her school. Somebody had built it in Minecraft, **brick by brick,** faithful in every element down to the placement of the chairs in

each classroom.

"I'LL SAY THIS ABOUT THE EVOKER KING," she said. "He has an excellent eye for detail."

Her friend Po Chen nodded in agreement.

Today he was dressed in an astronaut skin. "The Evoker King is *also* super talented at creeping me out," he said. "Because right now? **I'M FULLY CREEPED OUT.** Like, all the way."

"IT CERTAINLY IS EERIE," Ash Kapoor agreed.

"But why would he do this?" Harper Houston asked. "Why go to all this effort? There must be a reason."

"I know why: he's messing with us," said Jodi's older brother, Morgan. "He's probably watching us right now and laughing."

The five friends had been playing Minecraft for years. Recently, however, they'd started connecting to the game through experimental VR goggles. The goggles made the game utterly *real*. They could feel the blocks beneath their feet and the tools in their hands. **When they were attacked by hostile mobs, they even felt pain.**

What was more, ever since donning those goggles, they had encountered all sorts of strange anomalies – and outright strangeness – in the game.

And at the heart of that strangeness was the mysterious figure known as the Evoker King.

They didn't know who he was or what he wanted. But he seemed able to twist the rules of the game. **Many of Minecraft's well-known rules simply didn't work the same here.** And since they were *inside* the game, living it — that made him very dangerous indeed.

Some kids might run away from dangerous mysteries, but not Jodi. She ran towards them — sometimes she even skipped and jumped towards them. She loved solving a good mystery. It was lucky for her that Morgan, Ash, Harper, and Po all wanted answers, too.

"HUH, THAT'S WEIRD," Po said. He was leading them through a set of doors and into the gym.

"This whole thing is weird," Jodi reminded him.

"Well, yeah," said Po. "BUT LOOK. CERTAIN THINGS, LIKE THE GYM, ARE ONLY HALF DONE."

Jodi looked at the far end of the large, boxy room. **Po was right.** The Evoker King had filled the space with benches and basketball hoops, but there was no back wall. Instead, the gym opened on a view of the Nether.

Jodi shivered at the sight. The Nether was a spooky place, with flowing lava and floating bricks. In the distance, creatures moved across the red sky.

"Maybe he ran out of materials?" Harper guessed.

"Or maybe he wanted a giant doorway for a giant creature to step through," Ash said. "There are plenty of hostile mobs in the Nether. And some of them are big."

"JUST WHEN YOU THOUGHT GYM CLASS COULDN'T GET ANY SCARIER," Morgan said.

Jodi patted his shoulder reassuringly. She knew her brother had never managed to do a pull-up.

"Let's keep looking around," said Po.

They left the gym, went up a flight of stairs, and walked slowly down the hallway. Morgan peered through every window they passed. All the doors in the school had a little built-in window.

Well, not *all* of them. **The bathroom doors had no windows.** They stood closed. Jodi had the sudden realisation that anything might be lurking behind them.

"Should we check in there?" she asked.

Po nodded. **"I'M CURIOUS TO SEE WHAT MINECRAFT TOILETS LOOK LIKE,"** he said.

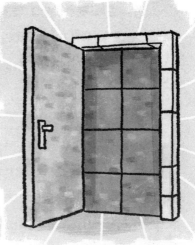

"As long as they don't smell too realistic," Jodi said.

Morgan pulled open the door. There was nothing on the other side. Just a wall of brick blocks.

"I GUESS THIS TOILET'S OUT OF SERVICE," Po joked.

"It's the same thing here," Morgan said. He'd opened the next door to reveal another wall of bricks. "This is supposed to be a supply closet."

"DOORS TO NOWHERE," Harper said. "Interesting."

"Did you guys hear something?" Ash asked.

"Is it the morning announcements?" Po rubbed his hands together. **"I HOPE IT'S TACO TUESDAY HERE!"**

"Shhh!" Ash said. Then she whispered, "I'm serious. I heard something."

Jodi pressed her ear to the brick. "I don't hear any—"

At that moment, the classroom door across the hallway shattered into digital pieces.

They all screamed, whirling to see a creature emerge from the shadowed doorway. It was a skeleton, but its bones were black. **It held a stone sword in its bony hand.**

And it swung that sword right at Jodi.

She flinched. But before the blade could touch

her, Morgan stepped in front of her. **He held up his shield and knocked the skeleton's sword aside.**

"Thanks, big brother," Jodi said.

"Thank me later," Morgan said. "For now, just run!"

As they ran down the hallway, classroom doors burst open all around them. **Skeletons stepped from the doorways,** each one black as night and armed with a sword or a bow.

"THEY'RE WITHER SKELETONS!" Ash cried. "Don't let their swords cut you or you'll fall under a wither effect."

"That sounds bad," said Jodi.

"It *is* bad," said Morgan. He kept his shield raised as he ran. **"THE WITHER EFFECT IS LIKE POISON. IT SLOWLY DRAINS YOUR HEALTH."**

"Avoid the swords," Jodi said. "Got it."

A flaming arrow soared past Jodi's head. Another struck the floor near Harper's feet.

"WE SHOULD AVOID THE FIRE ARROWS, TOO," Po said. "That's just a guess!"

"They aren't supposed to have those," Morgan complained.

"JUST KEEP MOVING!" said Harper and Ash in unison.

"We can worry about the Evoker King's upgrades to mobs *after* we get away from them," Jodi added.

They all hurried down the stairs, through the lobby, and out the main doors. Jodi almost expected to see the schoolyard's flagpole, bushes and fountain. Instead, there was the fire and darkness of the Nether.

And in the distance . . . **a cool purple light.**

"I see the portal!" she said. "We can make it!"
BUT WITHER SKELETONS WERE POURING OUT OF THE BUILDING LIKE KIDS ON THE LAST DAY OF SCHOOL. They launched dozens

of flaming arrows into the air.

Jodi jumped for the portal. Her vision blurred as she was enveloped in purple light.

When her feet touched down on the other side, her friends were right behind her. "That was close," said Po as he appeared.

A flaming arrow soared through the glowing portal. It nearly struck the visor of his astronaut helmet. "Too close!" he cried.

Ash took a pickaxe to the portal. **She knocked away a piece of the obsidian frame,** and the purple light was extinguished. "There," she said. "Nothing can follow us now."

"Uh, friends?" said Harper. "Anyone know what happened to our excellent undersea fort?"

Jodi gasped. She'd been too distracted to realise it, but Harper was right. The portal from the Nether should have led them back to the underwater monument they'd been using as a base. **Instead, it had dropped them in an immense, barren desert.**

Po let out a long, low whistle. All else was quiet and still.

Chapter 2

DESERT BEFORE DINNER! ITS TIME HAS COME!

A vast expanse of sand stretched out before them. **Morgan's head swam - if that was the right word when one was standing in a desert biome.** The voices of his friends filled his ears with questions.

"HOW IS THIS POSSIBLE?" asked Ash.

"Maybe we went through a different portal?" Harper suggested. "We might have been turned around in our rush."

"No way," Po answered. "We scoped that whole area out. **IF THERE HAD BEEN MORE THAN ONE PORTAL, WE WOULD HAVE NOTICED."**

"We all know how this happened," Jodi said.

"It's the Evoker King. It has to be."

A moment of silence stretched among them. Finally, Morgan sighed.

"Redirecting portals?" he said. "That is some madcap modding."

Ash nodded. **"IF HE CAN DO THAT, THEN HE CAN GO ANYWHERE IN THE OVERWORLD AT ANY TIME.** He can secure any resource. Move mobs around. There may be no stopping him."

"So why come here?" asked Harper. "If there's logic to his actions, I'm not seeing it yet."

They stared at one another as they each contemplated the question. When no answers came, Po said, **"LET'S LOOK AROUND."**

After being in the enclosed walls of the fake school, the desert felt huge. There were some low, rocky mountains in the distance. Everything else was sand and cacti. The square Minecraft sun was high above them. Morgan was grateful they didn't feel heat here or need fresh water. **In the desert, they were more likely to find lava than water.**

"Watch your step," he said. "No one walk in

any lava."

"LAVA?!" Jodi froze, scanning the sand around her feet. "Ok. What else do we need to know?"

As a fan of Minecraft's Creative mode, she was often surprised by details of

Survival mode. Many of the surprises were unwelcome ones – at least to her.

"Well," Morgan began, "you won't see many animals out here. Maybe some rabbits. **Hostile mobs, on the other hand, spawn like crazy at night.** We'll want shelter before the sun gets low."

"The good news is you can really see the mobs coming," Ash said. "There aren't many places for them to hide in all this flat, open land."

"OR FOR US TO HIDE," Po said. "I'm guessing we'll be building a burrow tonight."

"Like the rabbits," Jodi laughed. "You need a bunny outfit, Major Po."

Ash was still peering into the distance. "Is that . . . ?"

She gasped, then gripped Morgan's arm. **"EVERYONE TAKE COVER,"** she hissed, and she pulled him behind a cactus.

"WHAT IS IT?" he asked. "What did you see?"

"Something that doesn't belong here," she answered. "Do you see those mountains? Do you see what's right in front of them?"

Morgan looked where Ash was pointing. At ground level, there was a cave in the mountains. It looked like an entrance to a mineshaft. And in front of it . . .

"Are those vexes?" he asked.

Vexes were small, flying, ghost-like mobs. And Ash was right. They did *not* spawn in the desert.

"Three of them," Ash said. **"IT ALMOST LOOKS LIKE THEY'RE GUARDING THAT CAVE. THAT'S STRANGE, ISN'T IT?"**

"I think we left normal behind a few weeks ago," Morgan said. "And if they're guarding the cave, that must mean there's something worth guarding."

Ash grinned. "Then we should find out what that something is."

"Agreed," Morgan said. He looked up at the sinking sun. "Although it might have to wait. We should dig our burrow, set up our beds, and disconnect for the night. Then we can pick up back here tomorrow. Deal?"

Ash nodded, keeping her eyes on the distant vexes. **"DEAL."**

Chapter 3

THE ROBOT JANITOR ATE MY HOMEWORK!

The real Woodsword Middle School didn't have any skeletons lurking in its classrooms But that didn't mean there weren't problems

It was early the next morning when **Po realised something strange was happening** at the school. It started as minor annoyances. The automatic doors didn't open for him at the top of the wheelchair ramp. **The lights in the lobby's trophy case were flickering.** There was a low hiss coming out of the PA system's speakers, like faraway static.

He ran into Jodi, Ash and Harper in the hallway. "Have you two noticed anything

weird this morning?" he asked.

As soon as he asked the question, the static was replaced by the sounds of a chicken clucking.

"I was about to say no," Harper said. "But now that you mention it . . ."

Ash shrugged. **"It's probably just someone's idea of a prank."**

Po looked around suspiciously at their fellow students. "Speaking of pranks," he said, "do you have any guesses who the Evoker King might be? It has to be someone at Woodsword, right?"

"As a matter of fact, I've been looking into that," said Jodi. **She pulled a notebook from her backpack.** When she opened it, Po saw that it was filled with the names of their classmates. Beside each name, Jodi had written an observation.

"I noticed Missy Richenbacher spent ten minutes on her phone this morning," said Jodi. "But we all know her parents limit her screen time on weekdays. **So what is she up to?"** She flipped to another page. "And Josh Berkoff is wearing a purple shirt and a black jacket today.

He looks like a walking Nether portal! Is that a coincidence, or is he toying with us? Also, a jacket in *this* weather?"

"**Jodi!**" said Ash. "**Are you spying on our classmates?**"

"I'm spying on our *suspects*," said Jodi. "And, Ash . . . *everyone* at Woodsword is a suspect!"

Po shrugged. "She's not wrong."

"There has to be a way to solve this without digging into everyone's business," said Harper – and then she shrieked.

Po gasped. Harper was *soaking* wet. **A jet of water from a nearby water fountain was blasting her.**

"Make it stop!" Harper yelled, lifting her hands and closing her eyes against the torrent.

"Harper, just run!" Jodi said. Ash held up a notebook, blocking the water as much as she could.

Po launched into action.

He hurried over to the water fountain. **It was a fancy electronic fountain that the school's science teacher, Doc Culpepper,** had recently installed. Po knew

that meant it must have an off switch.

He found a big red button and, hoping for the best, he pushed it. The stream of water tapered off immediately.

But the damage was already done. Harper stood motionless in a puddle in the middle of the hallway. Water dripped from her hair, clothes and glasses. **The poor girl looked**

completely stunned.

Ash pulled a tissue from her backpack. Harper took it, then paused, realising it wouldn't be much help.

"**Harper, are you ok?**" Po asked.

Harper pushed her glasses up her nose, but they slid back down again. "Please tell Ms Minerva I may be a few minutes late," she said. Then she waddled down the hallway, squelching all the while.

Harper *was* late, but **Ms Minerva had other problems to worry about.** The clucking on the intercom had been joined by a variety of barnyard sounds. The class hamster's newly automated food dispenser was launching pellets across the classroom every few seconds. And the digital whiteboard refused to display the day's assignments. **Instead, it was showing photos of Ms Minerva's recent holiday to Mykonos.** From the looks of it, their teacher

had had a wonderful time on the Greek island.

"Oh no," Ash said at her desk. She pulled a dripping-wet sheet of paper from her notebook. **"My homework got soaked."**

"You think that's bad?" Morgan said. "*My* homework got eaten by the robot vacuum cleaner. It got one of my shoelaces and half my lunch before it was done. What's going on around here?"

Harper took her seat. She'd switched into her gym clothes, which were baggy but dry. **"I just**

saw Doc running from one disaster to the next," she said. "I offered to help her during lunch. She seemed . . . a little stressed."

Ms Minerva was still struggling with the digital whiteboard. She sighed at the sight of herself in a sunhat. **Then a hamster pellet hit her in the side of the head.**

"Don't feel too bad for Doc," the teacher said. "I have a feeling her 'upgrades' are the cause of these problems. Did we really need automated water fountains? **Or a miniature electronic treadmill for Baron Sweetcheeks?** He was perfectly happy with his old hamster wheel."

Po looked over at the tiny hamster on his treadmill. **All four of the little guy's paws were a blur of motion.** Was it just Po's imagination or was Baron Sweetcheeks sweating? Po decided to unplug the treadmill, just in case. The baron collapsed gratefully into a soft pile of cedar chips.

Ms Minerva pulled out a small stepladder. While she reached for the power cord to the PA speakers, Jodi turned to her friends. "We should all go with Harper to help Doc at lunch," she whispered.

"Sure," said Ash. **But Morgan elbowed her.**

"Don't forget, Ash. We've got to do that thing."

Ash looked confused for a moment. Then her eyes went wide. "Oh, right! We have that

thing. That . . . make-up quiz."

Jodi shrugged. "Ok. What about you, Po?"

"Po has to take the quiz, too," Morgan said.

Po didn't know what Morgan and Ash were talking about. But Morgan winked at him over Jodi's head, and Po knew he was supposed to play along.

"Yeah, right. The quiz," Po said, trusting that Morgan would explain everything later.

Unless there really *was* a quiz that Po had forgotten about. The way this day was going, it almost wouldn't surprise him.

The speakers brayed like a donkey as Ms Minerva finally pulled the plug.

Chapter 4

YOU SAY "POTATO." I SAY "DUCK!"

Doc was more flustered than Harper had ever seen her. **The teacher was wearing an overstuffed tool belt and a slightly panicked expression.** She kept dabbing her forehead with a handkerchief.

"I appreciate the help," she said, looking from Harper to Jodi. "This is too big a job for me alone."

Harper smiled widely. Doc Culpepper was her favourite teacher. That was because Doc didn't just teach science, *she lived it*! She had worked in a government laboratory before coming to Woodsword. And she still experimented in her free time. **The amazing VR goggles that**

allowed them to enter Minecraft were just one example of Doc's handiwork. Though Doc didn't know just how powerful her goggles were.

Doc had a reputation for letting experiments and inventions get out of hand. Even so, could she really be responsible for the chaos affecting the school?

Doc held up a clipboard. "Before we can fix the problem, we need to determine how extensive it is. **I've written down all the malfunctions** I've seen so far. But there are a few more areas to check."

Doc led them to the auditorium first. Harper knew the drama club used that space for their performances and rehearsals. She was expecting to find problems with the stage lights or the sound equipment.

She was not expecting snow.

"It's magic!" Jodi cried. She ran in tight little circles through the snow that drifted down from the high ceiling. "Magic is real! I knew it all along and *no one listened to me,* Harper!"

Harper stuck out her tongue to catch a snowflake. It didn't melt, but it quickly got soggy. She flicked it away.

"It's paper," she said. "Confetti. Special effects."

Jodi slid through the artificial snow. "Stage

magic is still magic!" she insisted.

Doc jotted a note on her clipboard. "The drama club spent an entire afternoon loading up their snow cannons. They are not going to be happy about this."

"Neither are the janitors," Harper said. **She kicked a little pile of paper snowflakes.** "I hear the vacuums aren't exactly working, either."

Doc sighed, nodded and wrote another note on her clipboard. "Let's move on," she said.

As they trailed Doc to their next stop, Jodi cleared her throat. "I know nobody wants to be the first to say it. But I think we need to discuss the possibility that gremlins are behind all this."

"Gremlins?" said Harper. "The little green creatures? People used to blame them for all sorts of problems, right?"

"I don't think they mean to cause trouble," Jodi said, her tone completely serious. **"But they enjoy riding the electrostatic fields of the stratosphere.** As you can imagine, that can really mess things up."

Harper grinned. **She had no idea where Jodi came up with this stuff.**

"I'm afraid there's a simpler explanation," said Doc. **"Human error."** She rummaged through her tool belt and pulled out a tiny computer chip. "I wanted Woodsword to be the most advanced school in the county. **So I networked the whole school. I put a computer chip in, well, everything.** And now *everything* is broken."

Harper's heart felt a little heavy when she saw her teacher so defeated.

"That doesn't mean you're to blame," Harper said. "It might be a hardware issue. Maybe the computer chips were faulty? Or it might be a software problem. **We could double-check the code that keeps everything automated."**

"Or it could be gremlins," Jodi added, her eyes shifting back and forth as if on the lookout for mythical creatures. **"Or bad unicorns."**

This time, Doc chuckled. "Yes, of course. It could be any of those things. Even gremlins."

The smile on Doc's face didn't last long. It fell away as soon as they entered the cafeteria, where the automated potato masher had mashed the day's supply of potatoes to liquid. **The automated potato scooper was splattering that liquid across the room.**

"I'll take things from here, girls," Doc said. She rolled up her sleeves, lowered her safety goggles, and walked boldly towards the potato bar.

"I've always wondered why she wears those things everywhere," Jodi said.

"Poor Doc," said Harper. **"This is every scientist's worst nightmare."**

"At least it's not throwing pineapples," Jodi said. She looked over at the students who were still eating their lunches. They had all crammed together outside the potato scooper's impressive reach.

"Hmmm," said Jodi. She took out her notebook. "Shawn Liptervoken is carrying around a tenor saxophone case. But I was *sure* he played alto saxophone. And . . . Hey!" She pointed. "There's Morgan and the others. **I thought they were busy."**

Harper shrugged and smiled. "They must have

finished early."

"I guess so," Jodi said. **But Harper saw her narrow her eyes in suspicion before writing something down in her notebook.**

Chapter 5

BURIED SECRETS! (BUT JUST SO YOU KNOW, ONE OF THE SECRETS IS SPIDERS.)

They returned to the game that afternoon.

Ash breathed a sigh of relief as her blocky avatar took form. She was standing in the desert burrow they'd built the night before. Part of her had worried that the school's tech problems might cause their headsets to glitch. But she was too curious about the desert mineshaft to wait any longer.

She could tell Morgan felt the same. His avatar rubbed its cube hands together. "I've been thinking," he said, "about how to handle those vexes. Or rather . . . about how not to handle them."

Ash nodded. **"LET'S HEAR IT."**

"We keep taking the direct approach," Morgan went on. **"BUT THERE'S ALWAYS MORE THAN ONE WAY TO DO SOMETHING IN MINECRAFT.** Why walk up to those vexes and get into a fight when we can go around them?"

"You want to look for a back door?" asked Po.

"I WANT TO MAKE A BACK DOOR," Morgan answered. "Also, why do you look like a rabbit?"

Po struck a pose, modelling his new skin. "It was Jodi's idea."

"LET'S FORGET ABOUT PO'S ADORABLE BUNNY EARS AND COTTON TAIL FOR A MINUTE," said Harper. "Morgan, you want to dig through the mountain?"

"Exactly," Morgan said. "If we dig through the rock, we should eventually intersect the mineshaft. Then we can avoid a fight."

"SOUNDS SENSIBLE TO ME," Ash said.

"Especially given the state of my sword," Jodi said. She held up a broken iron blade. "It shattered the last time I used it."

Morgan rolled his eyes. **"JODI, YOU HAVE TO TAKE CARE OF YOUR EQUIPMENT!** You should have said something."

"I'm saying something now," Jodi said.

"Why don't you sit this mission out," Morgan suggested. "You can be our lookout. Hang back and make sure the vexes don't follow us."

Ash knew Jodi wouldn't like that. **Morgan could be overprotective at times, and it always got under his little sister's skin.** If their avatars could blush, Jodi's face would be bright red.

"You want to leave me here?" she said. Her voice was strained.

"I THINK WE ALL NEED TO STICK TOGETHER," Ash said, wanting to head off a situation between the siblings. "If Morgan's plan works, **WE WON'T EVEN USE OUR WEAPONS."**

"And I can lend Jodi my bow, just in case," Harper added.

"Fine," Morgan said. "Just be careful, Jodi."

"Let's *all* be careful," said Po, **his bunny whiskers twitching.** "Like always."

"Let's gather our beds and make a few torches," Ash said. "We'll head out in a minute." While the others got to work, she pulled Morgan aside. **"HEY, GO EASY ON YOUR SISTER,"** she whispered. "For someone who wants to avoid unnecessary fights, it seemed like you were trying to pick one."

"Sorry," Morgan whispered. He looked like he wanted to say more, but he hesitated.

"What's wrong?" Ash prompted.

Morgan sighed. "I just don't want anything to happen to her. **WHEN THAT WITHER SKELETON ATTACKED HER YESTERDAY, MY HEART ALMOST STOPPED."**

"But you were there to protect her," Ash reminded him. "Just like she's protected you." She patted him on the shoulder. "You're a good big brother. But Jodi's a part of this, and there's no changing that."

"You're right." Morgan nodded.

"EVERYBODY READY?" Harper asked, taking a torch from the wall.

Ash and Morgan shared a look.

"Let's do it," Morgan said. **"ALL TOGETHER."**

They approached the mountain from the side, staying out of the vexes' line of sight. **In the silence, Ash pondered how strange it was to find those mobs here.** It wasn't just that vexes weren't supposed to spawn in the desert. They weren't supposed to spawn *anywhere*. As far as she knew, they were always created by evokers. And they only existed a few minutes before disappearing.

Since the Evoker King had named himself after the game's **magic-wielding illagers,** maybe he had a soft spot for vexes. That made a certain amount of sense, even if nothing else did.

It only took a few minutes of digging through rock to break through to the mineshaft. Their small tunnel opened onto a much wider shaft that ran like a hallway right through the heart of the mountain. **There was still sand at their feet and they were surrounded by stone.** But there were also oak columns, burning torches and broken rails running along the ground. It looked like something

out of an old Western.

Ash slashed at a cobweb with her axe. She picked up the string left behind.

"Maybe we'll get lucky and that's all I'll use my axe for today," she said.

Then she heard a hissing sound in the darkness.

"Or maybe not!" she said.

Red eyes glared at her from a dark corner of the mineshaft. A moment later, a cave spider leapt right at her!

Ash was ready for it. She knocked it from the air with her sword, then followed up with a second slash attack. **It hissed again** as it flared red and disappeared in a puff of smoke.

"Nice job!" Morgan said. "You didn't even need any help."

Ash saw more red eyes turn their way. "I do now!" she said. **"SWORDS UP, EVERYONE!"**

A host of spiders emerged from the dark. They skittered along the floor and up the walls.

"Where are they all coming from?" Harper asked.

"THERE MUST BE A SPAWNER NEARBY," said Ash. "Cover me!"

She ran right into the midst of the spiders. Her friends were just behind her, swinging swords and firing arrows. They were doing a good job of drawing the spiders' attention. **But they'd be overwhelmed soon.**

In the dim light, Ash almost missed it: a single cube-shaped monster spawner set into a corner of the mineshaft. **It looked like a cage with a small spider inside.**

Ash swapped her regular axe for her pickaxe. She swung the pickaxe once, twice, a third time — the spawner shattered!

But they still had to deal with the spiders that had already spawned. With no time to swap her tool, **Ash leapt into the fray with her pickaxe.** It worked well, particularly since she was attacking the spiders from behind.

Her friends were on the other side of the wall of arachnids. Morgan, Harper, and Po were all attacking with swords. **Jodi was using the bow** but seemed hesitant.

When an arrow almost hit Ash, she understood why Jodi looked so unsure.

"Sorry, Ash!" Jodi cried. "I'm not used to aiming these things."

"No harm done," Ash said. But the sooner this battle was over, the better.

"AGH!" Po cried. Ash saw the last spider had

pounced on him. **It sank its fangs into his arm.** "Help!"

Jodi drew her bowstring, but Po and the spider were moving around too much. "I'm afraid I'll hit him!" she said.

The others all rushed forward. Harper got there first, **ending the spider with a single swing of her sword.**

"Thanks," Po said. But Harper was already on the move, excitedly scooping up all the spider eyes that had been left behind.

Ash helped Po to his feet. He swayed, looking unsteady.

"I don't feel so good," he said.

"I think you got poisoned, buddy," Morgan said. "You should eat something."

"THAT WAS A DIRTY TRICK," Jodi said. "The Evoker King obviously put that spider spawner there."

"MINESHAFTS USUALLY APPEAR NEAR ORE DEPOSITS," Ash said. "I'll bet this is where he got the materials to build the school."

"He's probably long gone, then," Harper said.

"But we should still look around. If he left traps and guards, **THERE MUST BE SOMETHING HERE WORTH PROTECTING.**"

"That light," Jodi said. **"DOES EVERYBODY SEE THAT LIGHT?"**

Ash looked where Jodi was pointing. **Most of the light in the mineshaft came from scattered torches.** But there was a faint purple glow coming from around the corner.

Ash recognised that shade of purple. She ran towards it, trusting her friends to follow.

When she turned the corner, her suspicion was confirmed. **There at the end of the shaft was a ring of obsidian.** Within the obsidian was an otherworldly purple glow.

"IT'S ANOTHER PORTAL!" she said.

Chapter 6

WE ALL SCREAM FOR SCREEN TIME ... OR BECAUSE THE HALLS ARE FILLED WITH HOSTILE MOBS!

Woodsword had gone low-tech.

Doc still hadn't solved the glitch in the system. Until she did, devices throughout the school were unplugged and powered down.

"At least the lights work," Po said at the end of their morning class. **"Imagine if we had to do maths and reading by candlelight!"**

Harper nodded in agreement. But her mind was back in the Minecraft desert. Between Jodi's broken gear and Po's poisoning, they'd had to disconnect before going through the portal. *If* they'd even decided to go through the portal. Harper half-suspected the whole thing was a trap.

They had used dirt to wall off a little corner of the mineshaft. Then they'd set up their beds. That way, **when they returned to the game, they'd be right by the portal** and they could decide what to do about how to continue their hunt for the Evoker King.

Ms Minerva had wheeled in an old chalkboard for their morning lesson. As she wiped it clean with a tattered black eraser, Harper sneezed. She had never seen so much chalk dust in her life!

Over by the window, **Baron Sweetcheeks sneezed**, too.

"Well, that was adorable," Jodi said. "Harper! Take a video with your phone."

Harper sniffled. "Ok," she said. She put her notebook into her backpack and pulled out her phone. **She was the first of them to get a smartphone,** so she'd become the group's unofficial videographer. The phone was an ancient hand-me-down, however. She'd had to tinker with it to make it run more smoothly.

She opened the camera app and held the phone up towards the

hamster's cage. Ms Minerva had already replaced the treadmill with the old-fashioned hamster wheel.

"Come on, little guy," Jodi said. **"Achoo! Achoo!"**

Harper pressed the record button with her thumb. She held her hand as steady as possible. She was ready to capture the moment Baron Sweetcheeks sneezed again.

She was not ready for what she actually saw.

"Um. Guys," she said. **"You've got to look at this."**

While her other classmates filed out of the room, Harper's friends crowded around her. By their gasps of disbelief, she knew they could see what she saw.

She felt a small sense of relief to know she wasn't imagining things. But only a small one.

Because there, on the tiny screen of her phone, was the real-life Baron Sweetcheeks . . . next to a blocky Minecraft rabbit.

"Is that a new filter?" asked Morgan.

"No," said Harper, starting to get over her surprise. "I . . . I think it's really there!"

"No way," said Jodi. **She went over to the hamster cage.** She waved her hands around.

"You're passing right through it," Ash told her.

"I don't feel anything!" Jodi said.

On Harper's screen, the rabbit twitched its nose and hopped idly across the room.

"Follow that rabbit!" said Po.

They all grabbed their backpacks and scrambled out of the classroom. The hallway was crowded with students. **Harper had to hold her phone up to catch glimpses of the rabbit as it hopped between kids' feet.**

"This way," she said, and the others followed. But she lost sight of it as it rounded a corner.

"It couldn't have gone far," she said, and she waved her phone around. Its screen showed the

familiar hallway, **packed with students . . . and with Minecraft zombies.**

"Oh," she said. "Oh, that is too weird."

"Can they see us?" Jodi asked.

"Can they hear us?" Po whispered.

"I don't think so," Harper said. "They're just shambling around. Anyway, how could they get us even if they wanted to?"

"Is this only happening in the school?" asked Ash. "Let's look outside."

They passed through the lobby and held the phone outside the main doors. On its screen, Harper could see the playground. There was the flagpole . . . there were the bushes . . . and there was a huge ghast floating inches above the lawn.

"It's like a window into another dimension," Morgan said. **"A window into the game!"**

"We should tell an adult," said Ash. "Just to be safe."

"Doc will know what to do," Harper said. "We have her class next anyway."

"Aw," said Po , a little bit disappointed. **"I was hoping to see a mooshroom first.** It's been *weeks* since I've seen a mooshroom."

"Priorities, Po!" said Harper.

The bulletin board just outside Doc's lab was decorated with artwork. The younger kids had all drawn food webs, and Doc had put their creations on display. **But when Harper looked at the board through her phone, she saw something else. Something sinister.**

It was a drawing of a Minecraft Nether portal. It looked just like the one they'd seen in the mineshaft the day before. And it had a big red **X** over it.

"Oh man," Ash whispered. "**Someone doesn't want us going through that portal.**"

"One guess who," said Morgan.

"Or a few guesses," said Jodi. She was scribbling madly in her notebook. "Harper, didn't you let Sandy Mistletotter use your phone to call his dad last week? **And didn't you download a game that Tammy Yosemite recommended?**"

Harper turned the phone away from the bulletin board. Before she could answer Jodi's questions, her jaw dropped. "What is *that?*" she said. The hallway had emptied of students. But through the phone, she could see a tall figure in the distance, all the way at the end of the hall. It seemed to be moving blocks around. There was something eerie about it. "Is that a person?"

"It's an enderman!" Morgan said. "Don't look at it! Harper, turn away!"

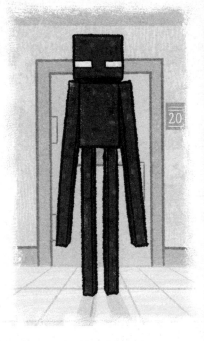

But it was too late. The enderman turned towards them. It seemed to see Harper. It glared at her with hostile eyes.

And then it teleported towards her. In the time it took Harper to blink, **the enderman's face was filling her phone's screen.**

Harper shrieked in surprise. The phone fell from her grip. It hit the floor with a *crack*. The screen went dark, and a piece of the phone broke off.

"Oh no!" Harper cried. She bent over to retrieve her phone. "It won't turn on."

"Is everything ok out here?" Doc stepped from the doorway of her classroom. "Harper, was that you I heard?"

"I just . . . startled myself," Harper said. **"My phone was acting strange. Showing us things that shouldn't be there. It was showing us Minecraft mobs!"**

Doc chuckled. "You five have Minecraft on the brain, don't you?" She tapped her chin. "But it's an odd coincidence that your phone would glitch when everything else around here is **crashing like two bumblebees listening to Beethoven."**

"Maybe it's not a coincidence." Harper's shoulders slumped. "Do you remember when you told me I could use some of your scrap for after-school projects? **Well . . . I may have used some of it to enhance my phone. . ."**

Doc clucked her tongue. "Normally I'd praise your inventiveness. **But it's a bad week to be using my hardware."** She looked at the phone in Harper's hand. "May I borrow that for a bit? Maybe it will help me figure out what's going on."

"Sure, but I'm afraid I broke it," Harper said.

"Maybe that's for the best," Doc said. "It's like my tech has developed a mind of its own. It's been downright strange."

"You can say that again," said Harper. Her eyes drifted to the colourful drawings on Doc's bulletin board, and **she shuddered remembering the big red X.**

Chapter 7

LOOKING FOR GROUP!
FINDING TROUBLE!

Jodi couldn't stop thinking about the portal.

If the Evoker King had meant to scare her away, then he'd made a big mistake. **Telling Jodi not to do something only made her want to do it more.**

She was practically shaking with excitement as she waited for the others to meet her at the computer lab.

Harper was the first to arrive. "I'm sorry," she said. **"I had to tell my mum about dropping my phone.** I told her I can fix it, but she wants to go to the store and have it fixed professionally."

Po showed up just as Harper was leaving.

"**Emergency basketball practice!**" he said. "I'll see you tomorrow. I'm already late!"

Ash had a scout meeting. "I can't believe I forgot it," she said. "Well, I guess I can believe it. It was a weird day . . ."

Morgan's excuse was the strangest of all. **"Detention?!"** Jodi said. "What did you do to get detention?"

Morgan blushed. "I decided to warn some younger students about the enderman roaming the halls. The teacher thought I was teasing them!"

"This is very aggravating," Jodi said. "I'm beginning to think the Evoker King scared you all away."

"We'll deal with the Evoker King tomorrow," he said. **"I'll see you at home. Don't go into the game alone."**

And that was Morgan's big mistake. He shouldn't have told Jodi not to do something.

At first, Jodi told herself she'd just play Creative mode for a while. She hadn't used the headsets for that yet. It would be nice to spend some time building without worrying about getting poisoned or set on fire.

But she and her friends were always in need of

more supplies. They could use more coal for torches and more feathers for arrows. **She still had to replace her sword.**

And if she was totally honest, she was a little annoyed at the last-minute change of plans. This wasn't the first time in recent memory that her friends had been too busy for her.

"I'll just connect for a little bit," she said to herself. "Gather some resources. That'll make everybody happy!"

Her avatar rose from the bed she'd left in the mineshaft. She left the bed there, along with the torch they'd placed on the wall. She knocked away the dirt they'd used to enclose the underground bedroom.

She poked her head out. No vexes. No spiders. Just the tantalising purple glow of that portal . . .

"I'll just take a quick peek," she said. "Then I'll come right back here."

She stepped up to the ring of obsidian. She reached towards the purple light. But she hesitated.

She thought she should leave something.

Just in case. **A trail of breadcrumbs.**

Breadcrumbs didn't exist in Minecraft, though.
She scanned her inventory for something else.

Seeds. She'd been gathering them for weeks.
She'd been hoping to use them to tame a parrot.

But they'd make a decent trail.

"So much for a pet parrot," Jodi said.

She sprinkled a handful of seeds at the base of the portal. **Then she stepped into the purple light.**

Everything on the other side was dark red. She recognised the landscape immediately. "The Nether," she said. "Not again!"

She was standing on a narrow ledge of red stone. **There was lava far below.** And in front of her, only a few steps away, was another portal.

She dropped seeds as she walked along the ledge. She held her breath and stepped through the portal.

She was back in the Overworld. But there was no desert or mineshaft in sight. She stood atop a low hill overlooking a swamp.

There was still another portal nearby.

"All right," she said, examining the new portal. "I admit it. I'm intrigued." As she stepped through, **she only hoped she ran out of portals before she ran out of seeds.**

After four portals, Jodi found herself in a dark forest. She didn't see another portal right away, so she walked deeper into the woods. She kept her eyes open for the telltale purple glow.

Instead, she saw figures moving beneath the trees.

"Uh, hello?" she said. "Morgan? Po, is that you?"

The only answer she received was an arrow. It flew through the forest, aimed at her chest. She dodged it and it stuck in the tree behind her.

"NOT COOL!" she said.

Sounds of grunting and honking came in reply. The figures sounded just like Minecraft's villagers. As they stepped into the light, she saw that they looked quite a bit like villagers, too.

All except one major difference.

They all had weapons. And those weapons were aimed right at her.

Chapter 8

MAYBE BENDING THE RULES IS LESS MESSY THAN BREAKING THEM.

Jodi was outnumbered. Her only hope was to make it back to the portal she'd come through. She looked down at her feet.

Uh-oh.

"Um . . . ," she said. "Any of you notice some seeds lying around here anywhere?"

The figures bleated and grumbled in reply. **They shuffled closer, raising their axes.**

"I guess it's a fight, then." Jodi drew her bow. "But would you mind standing *very* still? You know, to even the odds a little?"

An arrow whizzed by her head. It

came from behind her. She was sure that meant she was surrounded.

But the arrow struck one of her enemies, and Po's voice rang out:

"SHE'S OVER HERE!"

Jodi's heart soared as her friends came leaping out from behind the trees. Now it was a fair fight!

Swords clashed against axes, axes clashed against shields, and arrows flew from both sides of the battle. Jodi kept moving and focused on her aim.

"These illagers are no match for us," Ash said as her foe fell back, defeated.

Illagers. That was a new one to Jodi.

But Ash was right. **Working together, the team made short work of their enemies.** As the last illager vanished in a puff of smoke, Jodi beamed at her brother. "I'm sure glad to see you!"

Morgan did not return her smile. "What were you *thinking?*" he said. "You could have been hurt. You could have got lost!"

Jodi waved his words away. "I'm fine. I left that trail of seeds for you." **She'd been overjoyed to see her friends in her moment of need.** But now that they were here – and now that Morgan was lecturing her – she started to feel something else. "Besides, you're the ones who cancelled," Jodi said. "I'm the one who stuck to the plan."

"We couldn't help it," Morgan said. **"THINGS JUST . . . CAME UP."**

"Then how are you all here now?" Jodi said. "Did you all finish your plans at the exact same moment?"

"IT'S LUCKY FOR YOU WE GOT HERE WHEN WE DID," Morgan argued.

Ash, Harper, and Po were all silent. They'd clearly decided not to get between the siblings this time.

"I was worried sick," Morgan said.

"Well, I'm sorry I worried you," Jodi said. "I didn't mean to."

In the silence that followed, Jodi felt a rush of guilt. She really *hadn't* meant to worry him.

But part of her didn't believe his story about having detention. Or that he'd had a make-up quiz the other day. Part of her felt like the old Morgan was back. The Morgan who didn't want to spend time with his *baby* sister.

"We're all here now," Ash said. **"WE MIGHT AS WELL EXPLORE A LITTLE BIT MORE. Right?"

Jodi felt relieved to have something else to talk about. Morgan seemed relieved, too. "Right," he said.

"We didn't have time for sightseeing while we were rushing after you, Jodi," said Po. "Did you notice anything interesting?"

"ANY CLUES ABOUT WHAT'S GOING ON?"

Harper added.

"Nothing that made sense to me," said Jodi. "I'm sure you noticed that the portals go back and forth between the Nether and the Overworld. Almost like the Evoker King is using the Nether as a shortcut to access different areas."

"IT SEEMS HE CAN'T LINK TWO PORTALS IN THE OVERWORLD WITHOUT GOING

THROUGH THE NETHER FIRST," said Morgan. "So in this case, he's bending the rules more than he's breaking them. Maybe there are limits to what he can do!"

"Let's talk while we walk," Ash said. **"I WANT TO SEE WHERE THIS TRAIL IS LEADING.** And I'm guessing I'm not the only one."

Chapter 9

OVERWORLD TOUR! DON'T FORGET TO PACK SNACKS. ALSO TORCHES, POTIONS, WOOD, ORE, TOOLS, AND PORK CHOPS.

Po liked wearing his rabbit outfit. But he decided he needed to look like a proper explorer for what came next.

Their first stop was the Nether. Po hadn't missed it, exactly. But it was hard to argue when Ash called the view "breathtaking".

The group paused to take in their infernal surroundings. **They stood on a narrow ledge between two active portals.** Far below, there was a lake of lava. Across the way, too far to jump but close enough to see clearly, was another ledge with another set of portals.

The red mountains in this region were covered with portals. It was like an ant farm, with dozens of little paths going around and through the landscape. And pair after pair of portals.

"He's been busy," Harper said.

"I KIND OF ADMIRE HIS FOCUS," said Po. "I wonder if he's free for tutoring?"

Po meant it as a joke. But as soon as he said it, he remembered that the Evoker King was most likely a kid at their school. Whoever it was, they were doing an *excellent* job of messing with Po and his friends.

With every other portal, they appeared in an entirely new area of the Overworld. **They saw a lush jungle,** where Jodi kicked herself for running out of seeds to feed the parrots. They saw a mushroom island, where **Po spent a blissful five minutes chasing mooshrooms.** They saw a cavern, deep underground, lit dimly by portal light.

In each spot, they stopped to gather materials. The jungle had more wood than they could carry. The island provided mushrooms and mushroom soup. In the cavern, **Po breathed a sigh of relief at the sight of iron ore.** There was a lot of it right beside the portal. They would be able to craft Jodi a new sword and still have enough to replace some older pieces of armour.

While Harper smelted the ore, Ash looked around with a torch. It provided much more light than the portals, and almost immediately she noticed something in the shadows.

"What is that?" Ash said.

Po turned to see a small structure made of wood. It looked completely out of place in the stone cavern.

It also looked strangely familiar.

"IS THAT OUR BAT HOUSE?" Po asked. "The one we built on the school lawn?"

"Why in the world would anyone build this?" Harper asked. "And why here?"

Squeaking sounds came from the surrounding darkness. "Well, chances are good that there are a lot of bats in the area," Morgan said.

"LET'S NOT STICK AROUND TO MEET THEM," Jodi said.

"When the animal lover wants to flee from animals, you listen," said Po. He jerked his head in the opposite direction of the squeaking. "Let's get out of here!"

After another brief detour through the Nether, **they emerged near the peak of a snow-capped mountain.** They were so high that Po couldn't make out any details on the ground below. There were more mountains stretching into the distance, a whole range of them.

And looming above them, built against the very top of the mountain, was a house. It was large, wedged between two peaks. To reach the main entrance, they would have to ascend a winding wooden staircase. **Not that Po was eager to go inside. It looked haunted.**

"Well, that's an original design, at least," he said.

Morgan shook his head. "It's not. **IT'S A WOODLAND MANSION.** They generate naturally. But never in mountains."

"Another example of the Evoker King bending the rules more than breaking them," said Ash. **"HE DOESN'T SEEM TO CREATE MUCH**

ORIGINAL STUFF, DOES HE?" said Jodi.

"I don't see any more portals around," said Harper. "And evokers – real evokers – spawn in woodland mansions, don't they? I wonder . . ."

"This is his base," said Morgan, getting a flash of inspiration. "His home. It has to be!"

He took a step forward.

"Hold up," said Po, cautioning his friend.

"We've been in here a long time."

"We don't know what's in there," said Ash. **"WE NEED TO PREPARE."**

"WE NEED POTIONS," said Harper. "And cooked food."

Morgan sighed, but he didn't argue.

"For the record, I'd totally storm the castle with you," said Jodi, giving her brother a smirk. "But I have been known to rush in without thinking."

"Aw, the siblings do have a lot in common, don't they?" said Po, wiping away a fake tear.

"WE'LL STORM IT TOMORROW," Ash promised the group.

"Together," Morgan said, giving his sister a look. **Jodi smiled back at him.**

Chapter 10

I SPY WITH MY LITTLE EYE...A LIST OF SUSPECTS.

The next morning, Jodi's mind was racing faster than Baron Sweetcheeks on his hamster wheel. She sat drinking her milk on her favourite bench while her friends discussed what they'd seen the day before.

"The Evoker King has to be a student," said Ash. "I'd say we have proof now."

"I agree." Harper nodded. "No one else would be able to build replicas of the school and the bat house."

"Right," said Po. "It must be a student. **Or maybe a teacher..."**

"I'll bet it's that kid Theo," Morgan said.

"He basically swore vengeance against us after that coral jewellery incident."

"But that was *after* the Evoker King started messing with us," Ash pointed out. **"And after the sixth VR headset went missing."**

"And I really think Theo means well," said Harper. "He just went about things the wrong way."

"I'm just saying some of the teachers at this school could be secretly evil!" said Po, tapping his fingertips together like the villain in a cheesy sci-fi movie. "It's worth considering!"

Sitting in silence, Jodi had suspicions of her own. Her unspoken suspicions weighed heavily on her heart. But she had to pursue them.

She put on her large, lucky fedora. She flipped up the collar on her jacket. **She pulled her spy journal from her backpack.**

She slipped away while her friends continued their debate. **They didn't even see her leave.**

Her first stop was the front office. She greeted the headteacher's assistant, Mr Mellohi, and he smiled warmly in return. "What can I do for you, Jodi?" he asked. Jodi was always impressed that he knew the name of every kid at Woodsword. And she especially liked that he didn't care about the school's policy against wearing hats.

"My brother, Morgan, misplaced his science textbook," she said. "I'm trying to help him find it. You know, retracing his steps? Could you tell me what room he was in for detention yesterday?"

The man chuckled. "Morgan? In detention?" He shook his head. "Your brother isn't much of a rule-breaker. But I don't have to tell *you* that."

"Oh, I don't know," Jodi said, frowning. **"Sometimes people surprise you."**

The unwelcome surprises kept turning up as

Jodi followed the clues. A group of Ash's fellow Wildling Scouts told her there hadn't been a troop meeting since the weekend. **Po's teammate Ricky told her basketball practice had been cancelled** because the school-wide glitch had made it impossible to lower the automated hoops from the ceiling. She called

Harper's phone and got an error message. If Harper *had* gone with her mum to have the phone fixed, the errand hadn't been successful.

And Harper had joined them in Minecraft *after* she'd left school for that errand. Why would she come back so long after the final bell?

It didn't add up.

Or it *did* add up, and Jodi just didn't like the answer.

She wrote her findings in her spy notebook.

"Jodi? Is anything wrong?"

She hadn't realised she'd been sitting still and staring hard at her notebook. Ms Minerva's

voice brought her back to her surroundings. The teacher was wheeling the chalkboard down the hallway while holding a steaming mug of coffee.

"Why don't you help me with this and tell me what's on your mind?" the teacher suggested.

Jodi pushed against the chalkboard. It rolled easily along the linoleum floor. Ms Minerva nodded gratefully to her as she took a drink of her coffee. "Oh, sweet ambrosia," she said, closing her eyes for a moment and savouring the hot drink. Then, as they walked along the hallway, she prompted Jodi to start talking. "Well?"

Jodi sighed. "I think my friends are hiding something from me. **They keep telling me they have things to do, but their stories don't add up.**"

"What would they be hiding?" asked the teacher.

"I don't know exactly," Jodi said. But a pang of worry in her gut told her she had a theory.

"Maybe . . . maybe they just don't want to hang out with me so much. **They're making excuses to avoid me.**"

"Oh, that doesn't sound like them, does it?" asked Ms Minerva. "Why would they do such a thing?"

Jodi shrugged. "I guess occasionally I can be impulsive. I know it bothers Morgan sometimes. Maybe the others agree with him."

"Have you actually spoken to Morgan about this?"

Jodi shook her head.

"Maybe you should," said Ms Minerva. "You have a wonderful imagination, Jodi. But sometimes our imaginations can work against us. **We can often imagine problems that aren't really there.**"

"Maybe . . ."

"Well, think about it," said the teacher. "Honestly, I wish I could fix every problem you kids encounter. But that's not really my job as a teacher. **My job is to give you the tools to solve your own problems.**"

"Speaking of problems . . .," Jodi said. She grinned. "How much longer are we going to be using this old thing?" She rapped her knuckles against the chalkboard.

"Not a fan of the dust?" Ms Minerva nodded. "Me neither. But there's good news. Doc has traced the root of the problem to the school's security cameras. **An error in the software or something like that.** She should have it fixed soon."

They reached the classroom. Jodi knew her brother and her friends would be inside. She tried to act like she didn't have a care in the world.

But Jodi was troubled. Because she knew they had lied. And if that wasn't because they were avoiding her . . .

Then it was because one of them was the Evoker King!

She was sure of it.

Chapter 11

GIVE ME AN A! GIVE ME AN I! WHAT DOES IT SPELL?

Jodi had a hard time keeping her theories to herself throughout the morning. **She wanted her suspicions to be wrong.** But how was she to know for sure?

It was nearly lunchtime before she had a realisation. It struck her like a bolt from the blue. Something Ms Minerva had said suddenly echoed through her mind. Not the pep talk . . .

The security cameras. **The school had security cameras.**

She would be able to see for herself who had taken that sixth headset. And that person must be the Evoker King.

Jodi quivered with excitement. As soon as the bell rang for lunch, she jumped up from her desk.

Morgan started to say, "I can't go to lun—"

"Gottadosomestuffbye!" she shouted at Morgan on her way past him and out the door.

She knew better than to run through the halls. **Student hall monitors loved to exercise their meagre authority by calling out runners.** So she walked briskly until she'd made it to Doc's classroom. She caught the science teacher just as she was heading out for her lunch break.

"Doc!" she cried. "I need to know more about the school's security cameras!"

Doc chuckled. "Well, Madam Curie's well-balanced breakfast! **I do love to see a student so eager to learn!"**

Jodi huffed, out of breath. Unable to find her voice, she gave Doc a thumbs-up.

"As a matter of fact," Doc said, "I was just on my way to the security hub. I'm trying to fix an issue with the camera software. I'll give you a tour!"

Doc pointed out every camera they

passed on the way to the hub. The cameras were spaced every few yards along the hallway, higher than even an adult could reach.

"You must be able to see the whole school," Jodi said.

"Just about," Doc said. "There are a few blind spots here and there. Part of the gym, for instance. And of course, there aren't any cameras in the closets or bathrooms."

The hub was a small room connected to the main office. **Jodi marvelled at the sight of an entire wall of television screens.** They showed various locations throughout the school.

"I made two mistakes that led to the school's technical problems," Doc said. She slid the metal casing off a computer and **started poking around in the computer's guts.** "The first mistake was networking all the technology. That's what allowed the glitch to spread and affect

everything. The second mistake was using an old government AI program to run the cameras."

"AI?" Jodi said, her ears pricking up. **"As in artificial intelligence? The cameras are alive?"**

Doc shook her head, chortling. "Oh, no. Not at all. It's a very limited AI. It can't think creatively. It can make some basic decisions, but mostly it's just meant to follow instructions." **She pulled her hand from the computer to scratch her head.** "Although some of those instructions have clearly been confused."

Jodi remembered why she was there. **She needed to see footage from the day that headset went missing.** "Can I see footage from a particular day? It was a little more than a month ago."

"I'm afraid we don't save the footage for that long," Doc said. "With all these cameras? That would be way too much data for these old machines."

Jodi's heart sank. **So much for that plan.**

And then she looked up at one of the screens.

And her heart sank even further.

Morgan, Po, Ash, and Harper were there. Instead of eating lunch in the cafeteria, they were heading towards a supply closet. What in the world could they be up to?

Maybe they were *all* the Evoker King! Was the headset in that closet?

Jodi remembered what Doc had said about the closets. There was no way to see inside it. Not from here.

"Doc, I have to go," Jodi said. "Thanks so much for the tour."

"Any time," said Doc, and then she yelped as a circuit board sparked. **"But yes, it's probably best if I focus right now."**

![hammer icon]

Jodi sped towards her friends. She could see the door to the supply closet was ajar. **She could hear them whispering on the other side.**

She didn't want it to be true. But she had to

know for sure.

She threw the door open, shouting, **"I've caught you red-handed!"**

She might have said more. But what she saw took her breath away.

Chapter 12

SURPRISE! THE EVOKER KING IS . . . A LLAMA? WAIT, THAT CAN'T BE RIGHT.

It was a llama.

A giant llama. In the closet. Standing next to her brother.

"Ok, that . . . is not what I expected," Jodi said.

"Jodi?" squealed Morgan. "What are you—? You shouldn't—"

"Happy birthday!?" Po said with enthusiasm and confusion. He and Harper were holding a half-decorated

banner that said those same words. He added meekly, "A little early."

"You got me a llama?!" Jodi shouted.

But the llama's head popped off, revealing Ash, who smiled bashfully. "A llama costume, anyway," she said.

"It's just like a Minecraft skin," said Po. **"But for real life."**

"And it is so, so soft," Jodi said, petting the arm.

"I guess the cat's out of the bag," Morgan said. "Or the llama is. We wanted to do something nice for your birthday."

Jodi slapped her forehead. "Right. It's my birthday. Next week. Oh, brother." She slapped her forehead twice more. "I ruined my own birthday surprise."

"I told you she was suspicious," Ash said to

Morgan. Morgan nodded in agreement.

Po grinned. "Should have known better than to try to keep a secret from spymaster Jodi."

"I didn't think you'd ever find this closet, though," Harper said. **"Even the Evoker King left it out of his model school."**

Everyone chuckled for a moment. **But then**

Jodi's mouth dropped open. She reeled, and the room seemed to spin. And it was like the others could sense it, too. They watched Jodi as information started clicking into place in her brain.

There were no cameras in the closets. There were no cameras in the bathrooms There were no cameras in the gym.

The Evoker King had built a model of their school. That model was realistic in every way. Except for the closets. And the bathrooms And the gym.

"The Evoker King doesn't go to this school," Jodi said, her mind racing to catch up

with the theory that was forming.

"Uh, what?" said Po.

"He doesn't know what the school actually looks like. **He only knows what he's seen...**"

She stepped out of the closet. She looked up near the ceiling.

"**... through the cameras,**" she finished. "He can see this place through the cameras!!!"

Chapter 13

HOME, SWEET HOME! EXCEPT THERE'S NOTHING PARTICULARLY SWEET ABOUT A HAUNTED MANSION.

"We should tell someone," Harper said. "We should tell Doc or Ms Minerva."

"We will," promised Morgan. "We just need a little more information first."

"You think we'll find answers in that mansion," said Ash.

"I hope so," Morgan said, and he slipped on his pair of VR goggles.

In moments, they were standing on the mountain, in the shadow of the mansion. The sun was setting, and Morgan thought the building looked even more haunted than before.

"Let's do it," said Po. "Before I lose my nerve."

The interior of the mansion, at least, was just as Morgan expected it to look. They entered a grand foyer, a large room with several doors and a big stone staircase leading up.

"Which way?" Jodi asked.

Morgan and Ash both shrugged. "The inside of a mansion is random," Ash explained. "No two are alike."

"Just like snowflakes!" Po said. **"LIKE HORRIBLE, CREEPY AND POSSIBILY HAUNTED SNOWFLAKES."**

"I hate to do anything at random," Harper said. "But it seems there's no other way to explore this place."

"We should leave a trail of seeds," Morgan said. "So we can find our way back here." He smiled at Jodi. "I learned that trick from my brilliant sister."

"AW, SHUCKS," said Jodi.

Behind the first door, they found a room that was empty except for five potted flowers. They took a vote and decided to leave the flowers – and everything else they found – untouched.

The next room was all dark oak and **cobblestone** and held **a solitary jack o' lantern.** Morgan didn't like the way the pumpkin seemed to leer at them.

The third room was filled floor-to-ceiling with blue wool of various shades.

"Upstairs it is, then," said Po.

Upstairs was a maze of connected rooms, most of them **dank and gloomy.** All that dark wood made the place feel cramped and old. They passed through libraries and dining halls and bedrooms When they entered a room filled with cobwebs, Morgan readied himself for a fight. But nothing stirred from the corners.

"ISN'T THERE USUALLY A SPIDER SPAWNER IN THIS ROOM?" Ash asked.

"If so, we can guess what happened to it," said Harper. "It was somehow moved to that mineshaft."

"This place is way too empty," Morgan said. "Not just this room. We've definitely been through rooms **WHERE HOSTILE MOBS ARE SUPPOSED TO SPAWN."**

"I would say it's nice to have good luck for once,"

Jodi said, "but we all know luck has nothing to do with it."

The next room was the strangest yet. The far wall was a huge, pixelated piece of art. It looked like a giant illager head. But its eyes, which should have been green, were bright red.

And the room was crowded with people.

Except they weren't people. Not really. **They looked like Minecraft avatars, but they were completely still.** Lifeless. They sat at school desks and leaned against the walls.

Some seemed to be frozen in mid-conversation.

And there was something eerily similar about them.

"ARE THESE SUPPOSED TO BE . . . OUR CLASSMATES?" Jodi asked.

"It can't be," said Harper.

"Look there," said Ash. "Those look like they're wearing Wildling Scout uniforms"

"And the ones over there are wearing basketball jerseys," said Po.

"It's like the Evoker King is determined to build everything he sees at Woodsword," Morgan said. **"HE'S JUST COPYING EVERYTHING INSTEAD OF CREATING ANYTHING ORIGINAL."**

"Hmmm . . ." said Jodi.

"What?" Morgan asked.

"I don't know," Jodi answered. "That just reminded me of something Doc said earlier."

"How would he even do this?" asked Ash. **"You can't build an avatar using Minecraft blocks.** The hands are too small, for one thing. And the custom details of these outfits are incredible."

"This looks just like our team jersey," Po said, **poking one of the unmoving figures.**

"I'm not sure you should do that, Po," said Harper.

"Yeah, what happened to not touching anything?" Jodi said.

"I can't help myself. It's just too weird," Po said. **"BESIDES, THEY'RE NOT REAL."** He poked one figure in the shoulder. He poked another on the

nose. A third, he poked in the big, bushy hairdo.

The hair moved.

"Huh," said Po.

The figure suddenly burst to life. It darted past Po, who screamed and leapt backward. **Morgan screamed because Po screamed** and then they were all screaming, and the figure was running into the room they'd just come from.

Ash was the first one to follow. **Morgan came to his senses and ran behind her.** They twisted through room after room, punching webs aside and throwing open doors. The figure had a head start, but they were gaining on it.

I can't believe it, thought Morgan. *We have him. We're going to catch the Evoker King!*

The figure led them to a small cobblestone room. It was empty except for a cauldron and a brown carpet. **It looked like a prison cell,** with only a single door.

A dead end. They had him!

Of course, **there were no true dead ends in Minecraft.** "We have to reach him before he smashes through the wall," Morgan said.

But the figure didn't produce a pickaxe or any other tool. It didn't produce a weapon, either.

It turned to face Morgan and the others. It held its empty hands up in surrender. This didn't look like an evoker, as Morgan had expected. It looked like a villager. And one they'd seen before!

Morgan's square jaw dropped. **"THE EVOKER KING . . . IS A LIBRARIAN?!"**

Chapter 14

ANSWERS, AT LAST! AND LET THAT BE A LESSON: WHEN IN DOUBT, ASK A LIBRARIAN.

Weeks earlier, Ash and her friends had come across a village. It was a typical Minecraft village in every way, except for one detail: **each night, the village was overrun by a massive number of hostile mobs.**

They'd solved that problem. They'd saved the village. **And they had noticed, at the time, that the town librarian was a little bit unusual.** They had assumed her oddness was simply another difference that the goggles produced in the game.

But the librarian stood before them now. And she honked, **"HUUR ... I AM MOST CERTAINLY**

NOT THE EVOKER KING."

"Whoa," Po whispered. "Can villagers talk now? Was that in the latest update?"

"I'M NOT A VILLAGER, EITHER," she honked. "*Huur* . . . not really."

"So who are you?" asked Harper.

"'The Librarian' will do for now . . . *hahr*," she answered. Everyone was trying to suppress giggles. Hearing actual words spoken in the typical villager voice was . . . ridiculous.

"YOU'RE THE ONE WHO'S BEEN HELPING US," said Ash, making a mental leap while swallowing another giggle. "You've left potions behind for us. And the compass that led us to the underwater base."

"AND I LEFT THE WARNING . . . *hurr*," the Librarian added. "'Beware the Evoker King.' *Hahr* . . . you didn't listen to that one. But . . . ahh . . . he's hard to avoid."

"A warning?" Morgan said. "We thought it was a threat. We thought the Evoker King did that."

"**YOU HAVE THE SIXTH HEADSET,**" Harper said. "Don't you?"

"But why go to all this trouble?" Po asked. "If you have the headset, you're at our school. Why not talk to us there?"

"**BECAUSE THE EVOKER KING HAS BEEN WATCHING,**" Jodi said. Like Ash, she was connecting the blocks. "He's accessed the school's security system."

"That's right," said the Librarian. "**I'VE BEEN TRYING TO HELP WITHOUT DRAWING HIS NOTICE.** *Huur hurr* . . . I think I've been successful so far."

"Who is he?" Morgan asked.

"*Hahr* . . . I'm still working on that," she answered. "But I'm not sure you're asking the right question."

"What does that mean?" Morgan asked.

"Never mind for now," she said. **"HE MAY BE ABLE TO TELL WE'RE COMMUNICATING,** and he may be watching us *right now* so I'll make this

quick. The source of his power – *Huur* . . . I don't know what it is, but I've traced it deep underground. **IT'S LOCKED AWAY IN A DUNGEON AT THE VERY HEART OF THE OVERWORLD."**

"And you want *us* to go after it?" Po asked.

The Librarian smiled again. **"YOU'RE A GOOD TEAM . . .** *hahr.* And you're much better at battling monsters than I am." She placed her hands on her chest. "I'll do everything I can to help you when the Evoker King isn't watching. **BUT I CAN'T DO**

THIS FOR YOU. *Huur* . . . all I can do is give you the tools you need to succeed. *Hurr-hurr.*"

With that, the Librarian disappeared in a cloud of pixelated dust.

Jodi removed her headset. She was sitting in the computer lab and her head was spinning after so many revelations.

"I don't know about you all," Po said. **"But I'm more confused than ever."**

Morgan's frustration was written all over his face. "She said I wasn't asking the right question about the Evoker King," Morgan said. "What did *that* mean?"

"You asked who he is," Jodi said. "Maybe . . . you should be asking *what* he is."

Harper's jaw dropped. "Are you saying what I think you're saying?"

Jodi counted out the facts on her fingers. **"The Evoker King is not using the sixth headset.** He's able to bend the rules of the game, like he's rewriting the code as he goes. And he's great at building stuff – but not at creating anything new. **He's got no imagination. No . . . creativity.** It's the same with the AI program Doc was telling me about."

Harper hopped out of her chair. **"The Evoker King is like a ghost in the machine!** He's the ghost in the system! He's—"

"He's an artificial intelligence," Morgan finished. His skin looked ashen.

At that moment, a sound came from the PA speakers. Jodi thought it might be laughter. **It sounded almost - but not quite - human.** But it could have also just been static.

"Did you hear that?" asked Jodi. "Was that what I think it was?"

Her brother frowned. "I really hope not."

Chapter 15

YOU CAN BLOW OUT THE CANDLES, BUT DON'T CLOSE YOUR EYES!

Jodi's birthday celebration was simple. It was just the five of them, with no secrets and no surprises. Exactly what she'd asked for.

They were roasting marshmallows

in Ash's backyard. The fire was getting low. "I should ask my parents for more wood," Ash said.

"Allow me," said Jodi. And she tossed her spy notebook into the fire.

"Oh no!" said Po. **"Don't tell me you're giving up the spy life?"**

"I think I've outgrown it," Jodi said with a grin. "Anyway, it didn't feel right spying on my friends. I should have trusted you."

"To be fair, we *were* telling white lies," said Ash.

"We meant well, but maybe we shouldn't have done that when there were real mysteries hounding us."

"I guess it's a good time to give you my present," Morgan said, and handed her a package.

Jodi unwrapped it eagerly. She laughed when she saw what it was.

"Another notebook?" she asked cheerfully.

"Not for spying," Morgan said. "For *sleuthing*. After all, you solved the mystery of the Evoker King."

Jodi thought about it a moment. Then she nodded. "I suppose I did. And I can still be a detective without being a spy. I'll need a totally different hat, though . . ."

"Speaking of spying," Harper said. "Doc

told me it was safe to use her tech to fix my phone. The glitch is officially out of the system."

"Which means the Evoker King can't see Woodsword any more," Po said. "Whew."

"Probably," Harper said. "But we're up against an actual thinking computer program. I'm not taking any chances with my privacy." She held up her phone. **"I'm disabling the camera on this thing for good."**

Jodi grinned. "Should we say goodbye first?"

Morgan grinned too. "Just in case he's in there somewhere?"

"I like that idea," Ash said.

Harper handed Po the phone. "You've got the longest arms, Po."

Po held the phone up. "Everyone gather around!" he said. **"Selfie position!"**

They all stuck their heads close together. They put on their toughest faces. Po cleared his throat, then pressed the big red button.

"Are you listening, Evoker King?" he asked. "Can you see us right now? **Because we're not afraid of you, blockhead.**

And we're coming for you!"

They all laughed. Jodi enjoyed a moment of perfect birthday happiness.

And then she heard that sound again. Low, sinister laughter. This time, it was coming from Harper's phone.

"See you in the game, then," said the voice.

ISBN 978 1 4052 9552 9

The game is real . . .
so is the danger!

Four young Minecraft players have a secret. Their oddball science teacher's homemade VR goggles can transport them into the game! But now it's not a game anymore, and the new girl at school may be their only hope of survival.

ISBN 978 1 4052 9553 6

Bats are at large . . .
and so are zombies!

When a swarm of bats invades their real - life school and a zombie horde attacks their Minecraft village, a group of friends go on a mission to find out who is behind these monstrous migrations . . .

A map promises treasure . . .
. . . but delivers adventure!

When five Minecraft players follow
a treasure map, they find that their
underwater quest ties in perfectly
with their new school science project.
But trouble quickly threatens to sink
them in both worlds!

ISBN 978 1 4052 9587 1

MINECRAFT is a game about placing blocks and going on adventures. Build, play, and explore across infinitely generated worlds of mountains, caverns, oceans, jungles, and deserts. Defeat hordes of zombies, bake the cake of your dreams, venture to new dimensions, or build a skyscraper. What you do in Minecraft is up to you.

Nick Eliopulos is a writer who lives in Brooklyn (as many writers do). He likes to spend half his free time reading and the other half gaming. He co-wrote the Adventurers Guild series with his best friend and works as a narrative designer for a small video game studio. After all these years, Endermen still give him the creeps.

Luke Flowers is an author-illustrator living in Colorado Springs with his wife and three children. He is grateful to have had the opportunity to illustrate forty-five books since 2014, when he began living his lifelong dream of illustrating children's books. Luke has also written and illustrated a best-selling book series called Moby Shinobi. When he's not illustrating in his creative cave, he enjoys performing puppetry, playing basketball and going on adventures with his family.